The Littl[e Bear Who] Didn't Want To Hibernate

or

Even Bear Moms Know Best

Written by Bernd & Susan Richter
Illustrated by Sue Green

Published by
Saddle Pal Creations, Cantwell, Alaska, USA

Alaska, July 2011

This is the story of a little bear who thinks he is old enough to disregard his mother and to make it on his own. Instead of following his mom and sister to the winter den he decides to run away so he could be free. But he learns fast that this freedom comes with a high price, as he runs into one dangerous situation after another. Follow this little bear's tracks and learn what he learned the hard way, that is, how foolish it is not to listen to mom but to run away from home instead.

Acknowledgement:
We owe special thanks to Linda Thurston for her editing effort and suggestions.

Designed, produced, published and distributed in Alaska by:
Saddle Pal Creations, Inc., P.O. Box 175, Cantwell, AK 99729, USA

Other children's books by Bernd and Susan Richter available through Saddle Pal Creations, Inc.:

* When Grandma and Grandpa Visited Alaska They ...
* When Grandma Visited Alaska She ...
* Cruising Alaska's Inside Passage
* Grandma and Grandpa Love their RV
* Uncover Alaska's Wonders
* How Alaska Got Its Flag
* Do Alaskans Live in Igloos?
* Alaska Animals - Where Do They Go at 40 Below?
* Come Along and Ride the Alaska Train
* The Twelve Days of Christmas in Alaska
* The Little Bear Who Didn't Want to Hibernate
* All Aboard the White Pass & Yukon Route Railroad
* Goodnight Alaska - Goodnight Little Bear (board book)
* Peek-A-Boo Alaska (board book)
* How Animal Moms Love Their Babies (board book)

www.alaskachildrensbooks.com

To my parents,
Gisela and Wolfgang Richter,
who knew when to hold on
and when to let go. - BCR

To Larry,
who had faith in me
when I didn't. - SKG

This is the story of a young bear cub who lives with his mother and twin sister in the mountains of central Alaska.

As this story begins, the little bear, called Scruffy for his wild hairdo, and his sister, called Angel for her beautiful eyes, are still very young – not even a year old. Their home is Bear Valley and their favorite place to be in late fall is Blueberry Mountain.

Wolf Mountains

Hideout

Bear

Caribou Trail

Snowmachine Trail

Caribou
Pass

Coyote
Mountains

Monster

"Stop playing and eat some more of these delicious berries," mother bear encourages her two cubs jumping around in the middle of their blueberry patch.

"Soon we will go to the den for our winter hibernation. You'd better eat all you can now and store up fat because there won't be any eating while we sleep until next spring," mother bear explains. She knows how important it is for bears to have a thick layer of fat stored in their bodies to live on while sleeping through the winter. But her cubs are still too young to know.

"It isn't winter yet, Mom," Scruffy protests. "Why do we have to go to that dumb dark den so soon?"

"Don't call it a dumb den!" mother bear replies as she swallows a mouthfull of delicious blueberries. "The den is the safest place for our family to spend the winter. You have no idea how ferrocious and dangerous winter can be. My mom taught me that bears should be in a safe den when winter arrives and you better learn that lesson too. When you are grown up you can decide for yourself when to go to the den, but for now, you must listen to me and go there when your sister and I go."

"But Mom .....!" Scruffy tries to protest once more.

"I don't want to hear any buts or any whining, Scruffy," mother bear replies sternly. "Be a good cub, eat your blueberries and that is it."

"It's just not fair," Scruffy complains silently to himself. "I never get to do what I want to do."

The next day, the first snowflakes start to fall. Oh, what fun the little bears have chasing snow-flakes and catching them on their tongues while mother bear sniffs the cold breeze racing down the mountains from the north.

Mother bear knows that winter is close and that it's time to be on their way to the den before it gets too cold for them to be outside. A little bit of snow is no problem for bears.

But when deep snow covers everything there is to eat and when temperatures dip low enough to freeze streams and ponds, they need to be in the only good place for bears to be - inside a cozy den. "Tomorrow we will go to our new winter den," mother bear announces to the little bears as she watches the snowfall getting heavier and heavier.

"Oh no, not tomorrow already," Scruffy whines. He wants to complain again but he knows that he can't convince his mother to let him stay. That night, Scruffy lies awake for a long time, thinking how great it would be to be grown up and to be able to make his own decisions. If it were up to him, he wouldn't go to that dark den; instead he would play outside in the soft snow. He would eat whatever and whenever he wanted. He would go to sleep as he pleased and he would get up whenever he felt like. "I'm not a baby cub anymore. I can take care of myself," Scruffy thinks with pride. That night, he hatches a plan.

The next morning, mother bear gets her cubs up at sunrise. She needs to get an early start because she must search for a new den.

Last year's den was big enough for her and her tiny newborn cubs, but this winter they need a bigger one because Scruffy and Angel have grown so much during the summer.

"You stay here and eat your blueberries while I go looking for a new den," mother bear tells her cubs. "Don't wander out of sight of Blueberry Mountain. There are dangers lurking everywhere, especially at Monster Valley across the mountains. I hope to be back soon."

"I hope she will be gone long," Scruffy thinks as his mom heads down to Bear Creek and then east toward the Den Mountains. Scruffy decides it's time to execute his plan. "Let's play hide and seek, Angel," he suggests to his sister. "I'll hide first and you count to one hundred before you look for me, okay?"

"Okay, okay," Angel replies, somewhat surprised how eager Scruffy is to play so early in the morning and before breakfast. Angel starts to count and by the time she reaches fifty she's half asleep. So it's no wonder that she never makes it to one hundred.

You see, part of Scruffy's sneaky plan
is for her to fall asleep so he can run away.
He knows that his sister won't let him
leave without calling their mother. His plan
is working great so far with his mother off
looking for a new den and his sister fast
asleep. Now is his chance to escape, to break
free and to be on his own. This is the
moment the young bear turns into a runaway
cub. As fast as his short legs allow, he runs in
the opposite direction his mother his going.

He runs across Bear Valley to a point much
further than he has ever been. Scruffy
doesn't want to be found, and he is sure
that he won't be found here. Now he is a
free bear who can do whatever he wants
to do. "Life is fun this way," he thinks as
he chases more snowflakes and slides
down hillsides on his back.

Late that afternoon, mother bear comes
back from her search for a new den. She is

tired but happy because she has found the perfect place for the three of them. But there is trouble at the berry patch.
"What's wrong and where is Scruffy?" mother bear asks a squealing Angel.

"I hate him, I hate him!" Angel cries.

"Who do you hate?" mother bear asks.

"Scruffy, of course," Angel replies. "We played hide and seek and I couldn't find him. He left me alone the entire time you were gone. I was so scared, Mom," Angel sobs.

"Oh that Scruffy, always playing tricks on his sister," mother bear comforts her cub while holding her tightly. "Okay, Scruffy, the game is over. You scared your sister enough. Come on out now. We must go to the den before dark," mother bear calls. But there is no sign of Scruffy.

"Scruffy, that's enough. Come out right now, you hear," mother bear shouts again. But still no sign of Scruffy. "Scruffy, you come out now or I will drag you to the den by your ears!" mother bear yells with so much force that even Angel trembles. But still, Scruffy doesn't answer.

"Oh that rascal, nothing but trouble," mother bear growls. "Okay, Angel, let's go. He will come out and follow once he sees us leaving. He thinks he is so brave, but when he is alone he will get as scared as you were."

And so they are off on their way to the den. But even after they arrive at the den, there still is no sign of Scruffy following. Now mother bear becomes alarmed that something has happened to her cub. "You stay here at the den, Angel!" she orders before racing back to the place where she had left her cubs earlier this morning. "I shouldn't have left them alone!" mother bear blames herself as she follows Scruffy's tracks. She is afraid to find signs of struggle, thinking that Scruffy may have come to harm. But all she finds are the tracks of a single little bear running as fast as he could away from where she had left her cubs.

"That naughty boy," mother bear thinks as she realizes that her son has run away from home. "That foolish, foolish boy! He has no idea what he is in for."

While his mom is worrying herself sick over her runaway cub, Scruffy enjoys his freedom playing well after dark and only then notices the cold wind coming down from the mountains. "It sure is cold out here," Scruffy thinks as he finally lays down under a bush trying to get some protection from the fierce wind. He is so tired now from all the excitement and running.

But as he tries to get some sleep a strange sense of uneasiness overcomes him. This is the first time in his entire life that he has been alone at night. It is a creepy feeling to be all alone on a dark cold night. And it sure doesn't help to hear strange noises all around him. Wolves howl not far away on the north side of the valley. From beyond the mountains to his south and east he hears the yipping of coyotes on a night hunt. An owl swooshes right over his head as if it is checking to see if he could be a meal. And in the moonlight he makes out little shapes running here and there, squealing while being chased by bigger shapes. It isn't easy for Scruffy to fall asleep tonight. If he wasn't so tired from running and playing all day, he probably couldn't have slept during that first night all alone.

The next day, Scruffy is happy to see the sun rise. "That sure was more than a little creepy last night," he thinks, his body chilled to the bone. But the sunshine makes things look much better again. He is anxious to make his first day of total freedom a good one. His first instinct is to play with his sister, but he quickly pushes that idea away. He is on his own now and figures that an independent bear has more important things to do than play with girl cubs. So he decides to explore this part of Bear Valley unknown to him.

First he heads toward the Wolf Mountains, hoping to find some good blueberries on their southern slopes. He has learned from his mother that southern slopes have better blueberries then northern slopes, because they get the most sun. And the more sun berries get, the sweeter they become! Unfortunately, an increasingly strong and bitterly cold wind swoops down the mountain from the north, making it very difficult for Scruffy to be a happy explorer.

"Maybe it isn't a good idea to explore this side of the valley right now," Scruffy reasons

as he turns and heads to the south instead.
It is so much easier to walk with the wind at
his back, and even more so when he discovers
an animal trail made by caribou, moose, and
mountain sheep.

As he looks up the trail he realizes that this
is the forbidden mountain his mother warned
him and Angel about. "A huge bear-eating
monster lives across these mountains. I want
you to promise me never ever to go close to
those mountains," his mother told them in
a stern voice that meant business. She never
said more about the monster, other than
that it loves to eat little bears for breakfast.
This monster has always intrigued Scruffy,
and now, with his mother sleeping in a
far-away den, he is determined not to let
this golden opportunity to learn more
about it slip away. "If caribou, moose, and
sheep go to Monster Valley, then I can do
it too," Scruffy reasons. "What better
adventure than going on a monster hunt,"
he tells himself.

After a long walk up the steep mountain-
side, Scruffy reaches the top of Caribou Pass

where he carefully hides behind a rock to rest
and to study the valley on the other side.
Monster Valley is the most gorgeous valley
he could have imagined. It is bordered to
the south by the highest mountains he has
ever seen. In fact, they are so high that
during the winter, when the sun is low on
the southern horizon in this part of the
world, the sun doesn't rise above the peaks
for several weeks at a time. This valley's

meadows are at least twice the size of the meadows in Bear Valley, and there are blueberries everywhere. Through the valley flows a big river with enough fish to feed his family for an entire year. Along the river, Scruffy spots several moose eating twigs off alder bushes, while on the opposite side of the valley a big caribou herd is congregating for their fall migration. He can see all of this, but the one thing that totally eludes him is - a monster. There's no monster as far as his eyes can see.

Scruffy stays behind the rock for a good hour looking for any possible sign of the monster when suddenly he hears a deep-sounding growl. He yips and jumps up nervously quickly looking around where the growl has come from. Here it is again and it is coming right from, from ... his own stomach! Of course! He hasn't eaten yet and his stomach is growling for food. "I am starving," he thinks. "It's time to get some food into this belly, monster or no monster," he tells himself. And those blueberries are definitely calling his name now. After a last glance across the valley, Scruffy leaves his safe hiding place and heads down the slope to the nearest blueberry patch. "I'm in blueberry paradise," Scruffy exclaims as he swallows entire bushes of the best berries he ever tasted. The berries are so plentiful that soon his face, paws, and belly are blue from the ripe juices.

He is so happy about his discovery that he becomes careless enough not to notice that

he is being watched by two angry eyes.
Suddenly, an earth-shattering growl makes
his blood turn colder than this morning's
breeze. His heart sinks into his half-full belly
as he jumps up and turns to face what, un-
doubtedly, has to be the bear-eating monster.

But to his big surprise, he isn't face to face with
a strange beast. Instead, the big growl is coming
from another bear. Even though this bear is

twice the size of his mother and looks very,
very mean and angry, it still is only a bear,
which is a big relief to Scruffy who had feared
to encounter a giant dinosaur or dragon.

Obviously, Scruffy still has a lot to learn.
And the first lesson comes fast, as Scruffy
suddenly flies through the air after being
cuffed by huge bear paws.

"I can fly," is only a very brief thought
as Scruffy realizes that this bear is not in a
playful mood.

The moment Scruffy hits the ground, the huge bear pounces on him and, this time, hits him so hard across the backside that Scruffy rolls downhill like a snowball. Once more the giant lands right on him in a furry flash, cuffing Scruffy again and again. The two roll downhill some 200 yards before Scruffy is able to get back on his feet and to show his true strength.

Scruffy runs and runs the fastest he has ever run in his life. And that is what saves him. Although the big bear is incredibly strong, he is also old and has suffered a leg injury that prevents him from catching up with Scruffy's young legs.

After this narrow escape, Scruffy makes his way back to Bear Valley on very shaky and tired legs. He turns often to make sure that the monster bear doesn't follow and attack him again. He can't believe how close he came to being killed - and of all things by another bear.

Who would have thought that a bear would try to kill another bear? This valley may look like paradise, but now he understands why his mom calls this Monster Valley and why she didn't want him to go there.

After this frightening encounter, it takes all his strength to get back to his familiar campsite, where he finally collapses. He is tired from running, his wounds hurt badly, his belly is growling from hunger, and he is terribly cold as the temperature continues to drop. Altogether it just isn't fun anymore to be out here all alone. "I didn't know it could be that hard," Scruffy complains before falling into an uneasy sleep.

The next morning, Scruffy sobs as he awakens. "I hurt so much it feels like a mean old wolverine tried to drag me into a rabbit hole." He tries to get up, but his body aches too much. He feels weak from hunger after going without much food since the day he left his mother and sister. "I should have eaten those blueberries when Mom wanted me to," Scruffy thinks as he watches snowflake after snowflake falling down on him. Only a few days ago he and his sister eagerly chased and played with these snowflakes. Now, snow isn't fun anymore. Instead it has become a problem.

Scruffy has been resting in his hideout for most of the day when he suddenly catches the faint scent of another bear. You see, bears don't have great eyesight, but they can smell things from miles away. And now here is a scent in the air that tells him that another bear is walking around in his part of the valley.

"Oh no, not him again," Scruffy suddenly shouts, realizing that the big bear could have followed his tracks to this hideout. Scruffy urgently wants to get up now and run to the other end of the valley where, somewhere nicely hidden from danger, his mother and sister are sleeping quietly in their warm den. But he can't get up! He is still hurting too badly and his legs are too weak to hold him for long. There is nothing he can do but wait and hope that he is well hidden.

"I shouldn't have run away from Mom and

Angel," he blames himself over and over again before falling into yet another uneasy sleep. Scruffy begins having nightmares, which aren't nice at all. It was rough enough to actually have lived through the horrors of being cold and hungry and of being chased by an angry bear during the daytime. But what his body and mind don't need now is to experience it again in his dreams.

By next morning, a thick layer of new snow has covered the entire valley. "It looks kind of pretty," Scruffy thinks after shaking off snow from his head. This peaceful thought is interrupted by another loud growl, which fortunately is coming again from his belly. He has learned by now to distinguish growling of his belly from the growling of another bear. So he doesn't jump this time, but he is worried nevertheless. "I am so hungry. I need to eat," Scruffy reminds himself. He painfully gets up and slowly makes his way to his favorite blueberry patch farther down the valley. It isn't as good a patch as the one he had found in Monster Valley, but it is all his, and that's all that matters now.

"Oh no!" he cries in disappointment when he reaches his berry patch. A thick layer of snow covers the patch and Scruffy has to bury his nose deep in the snow to pick the berries. To make matters worse, it is slim picking because most of the overripe berries have been knocked to the ground by the cold wind and the heavy snow. Things just aren't going right for our little bear. And he still has that alarming sensation that another bear is roaming the valley and looking for him.

With hunger still gnawing in his belly, Scruffy heads toward the creek. "Maybe I can catch a fish or two, just like Mom did last summer," he encourages himself on the way.

Oh little bear, you still have so much to learn. Didn't you notice the ice that has formed on the creek during the last few days and nights? The river you saw in Monster Valley is big enough not to freeze up until later in the winter, but your creek is already frozen. There won't be any fish for this little bear. This is a tough lesson to learn for Scruffy. He had thought he was old enough to take care of himself and now he can't even find anything to eat.

But just when everything looks so bleak, he suddenly notices tracks in the snow made by a snowshoe hare. His nose tells him that the tracks are fresh, which means that a great meal for him could be right around the corner. Oh, how his empty stomach would welcome such a meal. As quickly as his feet allow, he follows the tracks, always making sure that he is downwind from the snowshoe

hare so it won't become alarmed and run away.

Scruffy is getting close to the snowshoe hare when he suddenly hears a loud and unfamiliar roar coming from the east side of the valley. Along the creek and racing toward him as fast as the wind blows come two of the strangest animals he has ever seen. Could they be the monsters his mother has talked about? Quickly they come close enough for him to recognize that these are people on smelly beasts that run faster and roar louder than anything Scruffy has ever laid eyes on. He had seen people on horses during the summer and he remembers his mother warning him that people are dangerous. "You must hide and run whenever you see them,: she had said. During the summer he simply hid in some brush, but now, without leaves on the bushes, there is no place to hide. Even though Scruffy is a good runner, it is impossible for him to escape from these beasts that glide over the soft deep snow because of his short legs and because he is weak and injured. This time he will have to stand and fight.

But wait, what is this? All of a sudden the beasts change course and head off in another direction! Scruffy can't believe his luck when he sees them now chasing another bear, one much bigger than himself. Could this be the big bear from the neighboring Monster Valley? "I knew it, I knew it," Scruffy triumphs suddenly. "I knew he was following me. But I smelled him from a mile away. He won't catch me off guard again, this mean old bear. Ha, serves him right that these people are chasing him right now. I hope they get him," he chuckles gleefully, remembering the heavy blows he received from the bear the other day.

"Boom! Boom! Boom!" The bullets fly
as the people chase the bear on their snow
machines down and over the creek until
Scruffy loses sight of them. Even though
the rifles aren't pointed at him, Scruffy
ducks every time another shot is fired.
"Am I ever in trouble ! What did Mom
tell me to do now?" he moans in fear.

He knows not to stick around, but to
start looking for a good hiding place, just
in case the people come looking for him
next. Oh how he wishes he were in the best

hiding place of all, his mother's new den,
but he doesn't know where to find it.

That night, Scruffy lays awake in his
tiny, cold hideout for a long, long time.
He is the hungriest he has ever been. He
is the coldest he has ever been. And he is
the loneliest he has ever been. He longs
for the warmth and safety of his family
and their den. "How stupid I was not to
listen to Mom," he again blames himself
before finally dozing off.

Scruffy sleeps for only a short time when something soft taps his nose. He ignores it thinking it is another nightmare, but when the touch turns into a bump, he knows he isn't dreaming. He is too scared to open his eyes, thinking that this must be either the people or the big bear coming to get him at last. Strangely enough, he doesn't care anymore. He feels so miserably cold, hungry, and lonely that he doesn't care what happens to him next. "Shoot me if you

want to or eat me if you want to – just make it quick," he sighs. But nothing happens; no shot and no hard blow from a bear's paw. Instead, there is just again this soft bump against his nose. He slowly opens his eyes and sees the outline of a big bear. "Mom was so right," he thinks. "He is a monster who doesn't give up before he gets a little bear for breakfast." But something is different about this bear. For one, it hasn't hit Scruffy like it did the other day. And this bear doesn't smell like danger. In fact, there is a familiar scent which is masked by the strong smell of fresh blood.

"Blood? I'm bleeding!" Scruffy suddenly shrieks. "Don't kill me, don't kill me," he now begs for his life.

Obviously, the hunger and fear have totally confused Scruffy's senses. He didn't hear the bear as it approached him, he couldn't make out the familiar scent, and he thinks he smells his own blood even though he isn't bleeding anymore! But instead of cuffing him again, the bear only hisses at him in a strangely familiar voice.

"Be quiet and don't talk such nonsense," the big bear tries to calm him down. Scruffy can't believe his ears, as he realizes that this isn't a monster bear after all. It's his mother! She has come to rescue him. Pulling together all his strength he jumps up, all excited to see her. "Mom, Mom, it's you! You found me. I was so scared that you were the monster. Take me to the den, please, please, please. I'm so sorry that I ran away. I will never do it again. Take me to the den, please!"

"Calm down Scruffy and, for heaven's sake, be quiet," his mother whispers. "Of course, I am going to take you to our den. Why do you think I came all this way looking for you? But be quiet now, the hunters are still out there searching for us. We must get to the den before morning and we have to do it while it's still snowing so our tracks will be covered by fresh snow. Otherwise our den won't be safe anymore. So, follow me quietly. We have a long way to go."

Scruffy's heart races in his eagerness to tell his mother how much he has missed her and Angel. But he knows that this isn't the right time for it. Now he must finally obey and follow her to the den, as he should have done days ago.

It is only after Scruffy has followed in his mother's tracks for a while that he realizes that the scent of fresh blood isn't coming from him but from her. He also now sees that she is walking with a slight limp. Suddenly it hits him that it wasn't the monster bear being chased by the people yesterday. It was his mother! It was she who distracted the hunters and risked her life to save his. Only she was smart enough to outmaneuver the hunters; something he couldn't have done. All the bullets missed her but one, and, fortunately, that one only nipped the skin without penetrating her body. Such a small wound would heal in no time. "I wonder how she dodged those bullets," Scruffy asks himself. "I have to ask her to show me next summer. I guess there really is still a lot I have to learn. If Mom hadn't found me, I probably would have starved to death or I would have been killed by a hunter or another bear. I'd better start listening to my Mom if I ever want to survive on my own."

Before sunrise, mother bear and Scruffy arrive at their den. Angel is sound asleep in the best place in the entire den. A week ago, Scruffy would have fought her for this spot, but now it seems unimportant to him who sleeps where. He is just happy to be with his mom and sister again. What he wants now is to sleep, sleep, and sleep. But his mother has yet another surprise for him. She pushes Scruffy to the very back of the den where she has stashed away a fish and several blueberry bushes, just in case her cubs play all day and

forget to eat before coming home to the den. This emergency food reserve makes a welcome meal for a very hungry little bear. With a full belly, Scruffy finally cuddles up to his mother as close as possible for extra warmth before he falls into a sleep that lasts the entire winter.

The following spring, Scruffy is the last one out of the den. That week he spent as a run-away cub had cost him much-needed energy reserves. In fact, he is now skinnier than Angel. But Scruffy has learned from his mistakes. Now he listens to his mother when she tells her cubs how, where, and when to hunt for different foods. Scruffy also learns how to sense weather changes, and he listens especially well when mother bear tells them how to avoid grumpy old bears. And, as all bears should, Scruffy eats whenever he has a chance. By mid-summer he has already stored enough fat to carry him through another winter of hibernation. By the end of the summer Scruffy is a big, strong bear almost the size of his mother. And when nature and his mom indicate that it's time to go back to the den, Scruffy will go gladly. He knows that next summer he will grow to be one of the strongest bears in Bear Valley. Then he will go again to Monster Valley to see who is the strongest bear of them all. But that's another story.

The Happy End!